A Land Called Grief

A note from the author:

If you are reading this with your little one while you are both navigating through your grief, my heart goes out to you. At the beginning of the book the main character Jack finds a crack in his heart that "...reminded him of someone he loved, someone he loved who is gone." This is a great place for you to bring up your own experience of loss, whether it be through death, changes in important relationships, or changes in life circumstances. Make it clear with your child that this little boy's loss is similar to their loss. My hope is that you can connect with your child through this book and that together you can navigate through your grief.

Dedicated to:

My Grandmother Elva - M.J.

A little boy named Jack, fell into a land called Grief.
The dark sky and bare land felt unfamiliar.
He had never been here before, and that scared him.

The fall left a crack in his heart.
The crack reminded him of someone he
loved, someone he loved who was gone.

Could this be a dream? He gave his arm
a little pinch, just to be sure.

"Ouch!"

This was not a dream.

Jack dusted himself off and tried to mend his heart.

He gathered clay and sticks, weaving it over the crack.
It made his heart beat slow and its size a little too big.
It would take some getting used to.

But then his heart dried up and turned into stone.
It was heavy. He set it aside, and his chest ached
with emptiness.

Suddenly, Jack felt mad!
He wanted sunlight. He wanted warmth.
He wanted color. Most of all he wanted
his heart back.

Jack started to wonder if being here was all
his fault. If he hadn't fallen into this land, his
heart wouldn't have cracked.

Jack thought that maybe, if he was strong enough, he could climb his way out of this land called Grief. He vowed to his heart that he would try his best to escape. So Jack started climbing up the cliff.

Jack climbed and climbed. But he slipped and fell, over and over again. He couldn't escape. Jack felt more sad and lonely than he had ever felt before.

So he cried,

and cried.

The land soaked up his tears.

And he cried some more.

Finally his tears dried, and Jack wiped his eyes.
He looked around and saw that the land had changed.

There was sunlight, and warmth, and color!
Beauty had grown from his tears!

Jack glanced down at his heart. He could see where the crack had been, but only a small scar remained. He now understood that his heart would never be the same, and that was okay.

With his heart mended, he decided to take care of the land for a time...

...gathering the beauty around him.

For the first time, since seeing the
beauty, Jack noticed a path.
As he followed the path, he discovered
that others were in the land called Grief.

The land around them was bare
and dark, just like when he
had fallen into it. He knew there
was someone they loved who
was gone and he knew he couldn't
change that,

but maybe he could help.

He decided to share the beauty he held.

Sharing sometimes felt like he broke
his heart all over again.

When someone felt mad, he made sure
they knew it was okay.

Some days, talking was all that was needed.

And other days, he was a
soft place to land.

Most days the best he could give...

...was a hug.

And through it all, they learned that a special
kind of love and beauty could be found in...

...a land called Grief.

Maddie Janes is a daughter, sister, wife, and mother who lives in southern Utah. She loves to read, write, and go on dates with her husband. Some of her favorite moments are seeing a bluebird, a garden full of flowers, or when one of her kids reaches out to hold her hand. Maddie and her husband have four spunky girls and one son named Jack.

Helen Bucher is a freelance illustrator and designer based in Switzerland. Her works tend to be playful, cute, and colorful. Besides running her art-related online shop and illustrating for children's books and other publications, she likes to play the violin, take care of her plants, and travel to Japan from time to time.

Made in the USA
Las Vegas, NV
06 January 2021

Björk
PRINT

Find activities and resources
for this book at bjorkprint.com

ISBN 9780578743257

90000

9 780578 743257

NCSM
Great Tasks
for Mathematics

6–12

Engaging Activities
for Effective Instruction
and Assessment that
Integrate the
Content and Practices
of the Common Core State Standards
for Mathematics

CONNIE SCHROCK, KIT NORRIS,
DAVID K. PUGALEE, RICHARD SEITZ,
AND FRED HOLLINGSHEAD

LEADERSHIP IN MATHEMATICS EDUCATION

NETWORK
COMMUNICATE
SUPPORT
MOTIVATE